BeastQuest
NEW BLOOD
ADAM BLADE

With special thanks to Allan Frewin Jones

Dedicated to
Aston Johnathon Briscoe

ORCHARD BOOKS

First published in Great Britain in 2020 by The Watts Publishing Group

1 3 5 7 9 10 8 6 4 2

Text © 2020 Beast Quest Limited
Cover illustrations by KJA Artists © Beast Quest Limited 2020
Inside illustrations by Dynamo © Beast Quest Limited 2020

Beast Quest is a registered trademark of Beast Quest Limited
Series created by Beast Quest Limited, London

A CIP catalogue record for this book is available from the British Library.

ISBN 978 1 40836 184 9

Printed in Great Britain

The paper and board used in this book are made from wood from responsible sources

Orchard Books
An imprint of Hachette Children's Group
Part of The Watts Publishing Group Limited
Carmelite House, 50 Victoria Embankment, London EC4Y 0DZ

An Hachette UK Company
www.hachette.co.uk
www.hachettechildrens.co.uk

BeastQuest
NEW BLOOD
ADAM BLADE

THE
ULTIMATE BATTLE

ORCHARD

MEET THE GUARDIANS

SAM

BEAST POWER: Fire
LIKES: The beach
DISLIKES: Being told
what to do

AMY

BEAST POWER: Storm
LIKES: Sports
DISLIKES: Injustice

CHARLIE

BEAST POWER: Water
LIKES: Puzzles
DISLIKES: Heights

PROLOGUE

"**M**y head hurts," Illia Raven groaned, pressing her forehead against the huge panoramic window. "I don't know what to do." She breathed hard, her pulse hammering in her temples. Nothing had gone according to plan since the moment she had hatched the Beast Egg.

From the high window of the Obsidian Corp research facility, she could see the clear blue waters of the Persian

Gulf stretching away to the shimmering horizon. The Dark Wizard Malvel had spent billions constructing the huge, egg-shaped building on the Dubai waterfront. But those Guardian brats had banished him, and now his resources were Illia's alone to use as she wished.

If only I were really alone.

She turned from the window and eyed the mass of scientific equipment that filled the open-plan laboratory. All around her, tech assistants worked feverishly at banks of computers.

Her head throbbing, Illia sat down at her own workstation and tapped at the keyboard. New data raced across her computer screen.

"If he keeps growing at this rate, he won't fit in the lab much longer," she muttered, chewing her fingernails. "And the bigger he gets, the more powerful he gets."

"*Feed me!*" A hideous voice scraped at the inside of her skull. A terrifying voice that had been in her mind ever since the battle with the Guardian kids in Egypt. Usually it was just a whisper – but sometimes, it roared so loudly, she feared her head would crack open.

"When that deaf girl smashed my Energy Crown, the link between me and him should have been broken," Illia muttered. "Why is he *still* inside my brain?"

A trembling man in a white lab coat approached her desk. "Ms Raven?" His eyes constantly darted up to the high ceiling as he spoke.

"What?" she snarled.

"I h-h-have the printouts you ordered."

As she snatched the sheaf of paper from her assistant's hands, Illia heard a hollow flapping sound above her. She glanced up just as Pox sprang from his lofty perch and swooped, leaving trails of green fire in his wake.

She stumbled back as the great skeletal bird landed on her workbench, sending her computer crashing to the floor as his talons dug into the surface. The Beast spread his

wings, a sickening stench wafting off his rotting green feathers. He had grown into a huge monster, with a wingspan of five metres. His eyes burned with malice, and a ball of green fire blazed inside his massive ribcage, sending tendrils of flame rippling out over his body.

The terrified assistant cowered on his knees. Illia backed away as the Beast's head lowered, the beak opening and unleashing a ball of green fire that enveloped the man as he writhed and screamed.

Illia wanted to look away, but she couldn't. She watched as the man's eyes filled with green fire.

Pox sucked the flames back into his

fanged mouth, and the screams stopped. The man stood up, his arms hanging limp.

Illia heard Pox's voice in her mind. *"Delicious..."*

The Beast flapped his wings, lifting his head and emitting a high-pitched screech.

Illia shuddered, sickened and terrified as the possessed man shambled away into a corner and stood facing the wall, his mind gone, his spirit feasted upon, and his body just a husk awaiting the Beast's orders.

Pox grew more powerful with every human whose life energy he consumed.

He's leaving me alone right now, but it's only a matter of time until he feeds on me too.

Pox sprang up, and with a flap of his great wings, soared to the steel perch Illia had constructed for him under the domed ceiling.

She put her hands over her face, blotting out the hideous Beast. *I should never have hatched him.* Tears sprang into her eyes.

"I don't know how to fix this," she whispered. "I need *help!*"

ONE

"Oof!" Amy was brought to a sudden halt at the top of the winding stone stairway. Charlie had slowed down and she'd thumped into his huge backpack. "Charlie!" she exclaimed. "That thing must weigh a tonne."

"Sorry," said Charlie. "The doorway is a bit narrow for it."

Amy gave him a helpful shove and they both emerged into bright sunlight on the flat rooftop of a tower in Karita's castle.

"What have you got in there?" Amy asked.

"Basic necessities for every possibility," Charlie explained. "Wet-weather clothing, high-protein food, water bottles, first-aid supplies, sunglasses, sunscreen, insect repellent, Swiss army knife, firelighters, torches, spare batteries—"

"We get it!" cried Sam, holding his hands up. "You're prepped for the end of the world."

Karita smiled, resting her hand on Charlie's shoulder. "It's good to be prepared."

"Or even over-prepared," Amy added with a grin.

Wuko leaped from her shoulder and bounded over to the parapet of the tower, chattering excitedly as he gazed out over the woodland and the rolling hills that surrounded them.

Amy knew that no one coming upon Karita's castle among the trees would recognise it as Avantian – no more than they would realise that Karita herself was not of this earth.

Although if anyone saw the light in her Stealth Panther's eyes, they'd know Varla came from another world.

Just like the hyperactive bundle of fur who Amy spotted bouncing up and down on the tower's battlements.

"Be careful, Wuko!" she called. Amy loved her Beast with all her heart; ever since he'd hatched, they'd had a bond closer than anything she had ever experienced.

"I've taught Sali a new trick," Charlie said, pulling a water bottle from the side of his backpack. His newt-like Beast slipped out from inside his shirt-front, her big eyes blinking in the light. Amy knew that Sali liked to doze in the dark warmth against his chest, clinging on to him with her six splay-fingered hands.

The others watched as Charlie poured a small pool of water on to the stones.

"Sali, dive," Charlie urged. The Beast plunged into the water and vanished.

Charlie lifted the water bottle and squeezed. Water sprayed into the air and a moment later Sali emerged from the jet, her six legs spread out as she angled herself in mid-air and landed neatly on Charlie's outstretched hand.

"Wonderful!" laughed Amy. "She learns quickly."

It was only a week since Charlie's strange little Beast had emerged from her egg, but – after a slightly tricky start – the bond between Guardian and Beast had quickly formed.

"Stretch your wings, Spark!" Sam said. The little dragon opened its silvery wings and soared up into the clear sky, circling the castle and crying in her shrill voice.

"She loves flying free," Sam said affectionately. "She doesn't get out much back home – even small dragons would create chaos if they were spotted in the middle of London."

"Indeed," said Karita, leaning on her long bo-staff as she watched the dragon wheeling through the air. "It is a shame that our Beasts must be kept hidden in this world." Amy recognised the faraway look in her eyes.

She's thinking of Avantia. Amy knew how much Karita missed her homeland – but as long as danger threatened Earth, she felt a duty to remain.

Karita looked thoughtfully at the three Guardians. "You have all told your parents they will not be able to contact you for this weekend?" she asked.

Amy nodded. "I've said the school trip will take us where there's no mobile phone reception," she affirmed.

"Which is true," added Sam. "Although the place we're heading for is a whole lot further away than my mom thinks."

"What's Avantia like?" Charlie asked, posing a question that Amy had been pondering for days.

"In many ways, it is very similar to Earth," said Karita. Then she frowned. "And in some ways, very different." She looked from one to the other. "Call your Beasts back, Guardians – we must open the portal."

Amy felt a shiver run down her spine as she beckoned Wuko to come down off the battlements. Karita had already explained to them that they would need help to defeat Illia Raven and her newly hatched Beast, a hideous skeletal phoenix she had named Pox. And that help could only come from Avantia.

They'd opened a portal once before, on Malvel's yacht, the *Torgor*. They had gathered around Karita as she held Gustav of Colwyn's mysterious compass up high, the Guardians' Arcane Bands fuelling the device's magical power.

When the dark portal had opened they'd pushed Malvel through. But Illia, Malvel's human ally, had escaped.

I wish we'd shoved her through at the same time! That would have saved us a lot of trouble. Amy shuddered. *Now she has that horrible Beast with her, and she's as big a threat as Malvel ever was.*

Karita stood in the centre of the turret's stone roof, Varla pressing close to her side. Amy, Charlie and Sam gathered around her, facing inwards. Spark perched on Sam's shoulder, Wuko clung to Amy's neck, and Sali slipped into Charlie's shirt-front so that only her big, blinking eyes were visible.

Karita took the precious compass from a

pocket and held it up.

Amy felt her Arcane Band tingling on her wrist as she lifted her arm. Charlie and Sam did the same.

The air hummed, Amy's hearing implants filling her head with a buzzing that was like angry hornets. She felt as though she had lightning in her veins. The woodlands around the castle blurred. The stones quivered under her feet.

"It is time!" cried Karita. She pressed the centre of the compass.

There was a sound like thunder as a fire-rimmed hole appeared right behind Sam. The portal grew, spitting sparks like a firework. At its heart was a deep blackness.

"Brave hearts, Guardians!" called Karita. "To Avantia!"

Her brain on fire and her heart hammering, Amy followed the others over the blazing threshold into the gaping nothingness.

She gasped.

They were standing on a high, rock-strewn slope halfway up a towering mountain. All around them, cracks spewed greenish steam that boiled into the red-tinged sky. The reek of sulphur tightened Amy's throat, making her cough.

"Well, this isn't good," choked Sam. "Where are all the fields and rivers and cute little villages?"

Karita gazed around at the desolate mountainside. "I do not know this place," she said, her voice catching from the sulphur.

"I do," said Charlie. "It's a volcano!"

"Are we even *in* Avantia?" Amy wheezed, feeling Wuko's fingers digging into her skin. He was as alarmed as her by their surroundings.

"Avantia has mountain ranges to the north and the east," Karita replied. "But I have not been here in many years – I need a moment to think."

A sudden movement caught Amy's eye. Was there something hiding among the rocks?

The grate and grind of stone on stone made everyone turn. Rocks and boulders slid together, mingling with gravel and sand, piling themselves into a mound.

"What on Earth...?" began Charlie.

"Not on *Earth*," Sam broke in. "Not on Earth at all!"

Amy watched, hardly breathing, the hairs prickling on her neck, a hollow sensation yawning in her stomach. The rocks continued piling one on to another, the lumpen shape rising high above them, forming legs and a torso, and thick, powerful arms.

A huge boulder clamped down on to the top of the monstrous body. It had a crack across it, like the slash of a mouth, and two dark pits that opened to reveal cruel, white eyes.

"*Grarrrrggh!*"

With a guttural roar, the rock monster lurched forwards, its massive stone fist heading right for them.

TWO

Sam leaped backwards to avoid the rock monster's swinging fist.

"It's a shardling!" cried Karita, bounding back, her bo-staff spinning in her hands. "An Avantian mountain demon! Don't let it touch you!"

Sam activated his Arcane Band. The chain reeled out from his wrist, the hook cutting through the air.

That thing's got hands the size of

wrecking balls!

Spark took to the air, shrieking and spitting fire.

On either side, Sam saw Amy and Charlie running to encircle the monster: Amy with her spiked club in both hands, Charlie hefting his silver axe.

Karita bounded forwards, hammering her bo-staff into the ground and using it to propel herself into the air. She drove her feet into the monster's face, knocking it backwards. Varla pounced, her huge claws raking the thing's broad chest, keeping it off-balance.

"Bring it down!" Sam shouted, whirling his hook and chain around his head and then flinging it to tangle around the shardling's legs. Charlie and Amy also closed in, beating at the monster's legs with axe and club.

It stumbled, arms flailing. Sam saw Wuko clinging to the monster's neck, his hands glowing as he drew out its energy and power.

Sam dug his heels in, hauling back on his chain, hoping to topple the monster. But it was too strong, and before Sam could dive out of the way, a massive hand closed around his body, lifting him into the air.

Spark was there in an instant, breathing fire over the shardling's wrist. Sam winced as the stone fingers grew hot around his body. But his Beast's licking flames couldn't harm him – and he saw that the gravel and sand that glued the shardling's body together was melting, and turning glassy in the heat.

"Hit its arm!" Sam shouted to the others.

Stone might be tough, but glass sure isn't!

Charlie jumped high, bringing his axe down on the glassy wrist. The stones burst apart, the fingers loosening enough for Sam to leap down, and land nimbly on his feet. The monster reeled back, roaring as its severed hand crashed to the ground, the fingers falling to pieces.

"Spark! Do that again!" Sam shouted.

Wuko was on the monster's head now, his hands spread to cover its eyes. Karita, Varla,

Amy and Charlie circled it while Spark darted in and out, spraying the creature with fire as it lurched about blindly.

And every time Spark's flames burned the gravel and sand to glass, the Guardians were there – hacking at the monster's body until the shardling fell forwards, smashing into fragments that scattered across the ground.

"Well, that wasn't so hard," panted Charlie, leaning on his axe.

"Guardians, one – Rocky, zero," added Sam.

"Do not be fooled," warned Karita. "Shardlings have the power to reassemble themselves – we must get away from here before that happens."

"I second that," said Amy, stroking Wuko's fur as he nestled against her neck. "You were very brave," she told him. "But I wish you wouldn't put yourself into danger quite so often." Wuko grinned at her and chattered excitedly. "Yes, I know it's fun," Amy said. "But you need to be more careful."

"As must we all," agreed Karita. "Come – I think I know where we are."

They followed her down the long barren slope of the mountain, Spark perched on Sam's cap, Wuko on Amy's shoulder and Sali – as usual – in Charlie's shirt.

After a while, the air began to clear, and Sam found he could breathe without the sulphur irritating his nose and throat.

He looked back. The head of the conical mountain was covered by a cap of greenish-grey smoke, but the rest of the sky was blue. Below them, a great green landscape spread almost to the horizon. In the far distance was a forest, and over to the left something silvery. *A lake, maybe?*

"Yes," said Karita, breathing deeply on the clean air. "This is Stonewin Volcano."

Sam stared at her in surprise. "Stonewin? That's my surname!"

"Indeed, Sam," Karita replied. "You are a descendant of the Stonewins of Avantia." She pointed into the distance. "There lies Lake Rokston, where I often swam as a child." She moved her finger. "And there are the Grassy Plains. The City stands on their southernmost edge, close to the Winding River that empties into the great Western Ocean." She sighed, tears in her eyes. "It is good to see my homeland again after so many years."

"I think I see the City," said Amy, pointing to a spot where something twinkled and glinted.

"That is the sunlight reflecting off the towers of King Hugo's Palace," said Karita. "The sooner we present ourselves to the king, the sooner we shall find the help we seek."

She strode down the slope, Varla gliding

alongside and the Guardians following. All three of them stared around in wonderment.

"Some of our grandparents came from here," said Charlie. "Isn't that totally amazing?"

"It's pretty awesome," agreed Sam.

"It's hard to take in," added Amy. "But I almost feel at home here, as if—"

A deafening grinding and cracking noise cut her off. Smoke gushed up all around them as a whole stretch of the mountainside fell away under their feet.

Sam was thrown on to his back as the smoke engulfed him. Instinctively, he brought his Arcane Band to life and dug the hook deep into the ground. "Hang on to me!" he yelled.

Charlie and Amy clung to him as the ground tilted down into a deep chasm filled with thick, churning clouds of smoke, lit from below with a vivid, orange glare.

With a bone-shaking shudder, the shelf of rock became still. Sam stared down. Varla had dug her great claws into the ground and was hanging there, Karita holding on to her in turn.

Overpowering heat struck up at them.

Charlie let out a cry. "No, no, no! *Noooo!*" He clutched frantically as his backpack slid away and plunged into the chasm.

So much for being prepared for anything,

Sam thought grimly.

As the smoke cleared, he stared down in horror.

The fierce orange light came from a chamber that bubbled and seethed with a sea of liquid magma. They were staring into the very heart of the volcano!

"Is everyone all right?" Karita called up to them.

"I think so," Amy gasped.

"Use all your skills, Guardians," Karita called. "Climb to safe ground."

Sam got carefully to his feet. He looked upwards. That was easier said than done – the entire shelf of rock they were on had collapsed below ground level.

And that wasn't the worst news.

As Sam looked more closely at the sheer cavern walls, he saw things moving.

Rocks and boulders gathered all round them in a slurry of sand and grit. Shapes were already beginning to form...semi-human shapes.

"Shardlings!" Sam yelled. "Everywhere! Dozens of them!"

And even as his voice echoed through the chamber, the shardlings shuddered into life and shambled towards the Guardians.

THREE

Charlie's face ran with sweat, his heart pounding against his ribs as he imagined how close he and Sali had come to following his backpack on that terrible fall down into the heaving and bubbling magma.

The heat struck up at them with the force of an open furnace, and the air was thick with sulphurous steams.

And more shardlings!

"Make for safer ground!" shouted Karita. She and Varla scrambled across the tilted face of the collapsing rock shelf – heading towards a stony outcrop jutting from the cavern's sheer wall.

Shardlings lurched in from all sides, their great fingers and feet digging into the walls as they edged closer.

Charlie ran, one hand pressed against his shirt-front to make sure Sali was safe. Sam and Amy ran alongside him, Wuko bounding out in front, Spark flying over Sam's head.

A terrible noise reverberated through the cavern as the rock shelf slid away under them. Karita and Varla were already on the outcrop, Karita at the very edge, urging them on.

A gap opened between them and safe ground.

Amy leaped and Karita caught her.

The ground tilted wildly, throwing Charlie on to his face. Sam grabbed his arm and dragged him upright.

"Let's do this together," Sam gasped. "Ready?"

Charlie nodded and they ran the final stretch. Shardlings were closing in along the walls. There was a thunderous boom and a bone-shaking crash.

"Jump!" yelled Sam.

The rock fell away under Charlie's feet

as he propelled himself into the air, Sam's fingers tightening on his arm.

Molten rock bubbled and spat beneath them. Heat blasted up.

Charlie and Sam landed on solid stone. Amy and Karita grabbed them just as the rock shelf they'd jumped from slid down into the magma. There was a deafening, roaring hiss and fountains of magma spurted up as the shelf was engulfed by molten rock.

That was way too close...

"Stand firm, Guardians!" shouted Karita, swinging her bo-staff at the closest of the shardlings. For the moment they were safe from the magma, but Charlie couldn't see how they were going to get back to the surface. "While there is breath in our lungs, we must fight!"

Shardlings surrounded them, jumping down from above, climbing up from below and edging in along the walls.

Charlie held his axe in both hands, his blood thundering in his head. Spark zipped through the air. She seemed to be everywhere at once, like a silver missile, spraying the monsters with blasts of fierce flame.

Charlie swung his axe, aiming for a glassy patch at a shardling's elbow. The arm splintered and thumped to the ground. Charlie saw another glassy clump in the shardling's chest. He swung his axe with all his strength, burying the blade in the monster's chest. He fought to pull it out, but it was tightly wedged. He saw a flash of movement, and suddenly, Varla and Karita were at his side. Varla leaped up, raking at the shardling's eyes. It tried to ward the Stealth Panther off with its one remaining arm, but – almost quicker than Charlie could follow – Varla slipped around the monster's back, clawing at its neck with razor-sharp talons.

Karita hammered the end of her bo-staff into the crack where Charlie's axe-head was lodged. She leaped sideways, prising the rocks apart.

Charlie lurched backwards as his axe sprang free.

"Now!" Karita cried.

Charlie hacked the blade deep into the open cleft. The shardling let out a roar as its chest broke open, the crumbling rocks spilling and tumbling all around Charlie as he jumped to safety.

One down!

He stared around, panting. Spark was causing mayhem among the shardlings, flying in low, spitting fire, then jinking out of reach.

Sam and Amy were darting under pounding fists, Amy's mace cracking rocks and Sam's hook ripping stones apart.

Fragments of glass cascaded down like hailstones.

Wuko leaped from monster to monster, pressing his hands down on to their lumpy shoulders and heads, sapping their energy and loosening the bonds that held their bodies together.

Charlie stared at Karita and Varla, amazed. One moment, they were attacking a monster from in front; a split second later, they were at its back, claws and fangs raking the stones, Karita's bo-staff finding glassy crevices to prise apart.

That's Stealth Powers for you!

Charlie felt Sali thumping his chest with all six feet.

It was a warning signal.

He heard the crunch of heavy feet behind him. He turned, lifting his axe, but the towering shardling closed its huge stone fingers around his arm before he could take aim. He was lifted into the air, struggling and kicking.

Charlie kicked wildly. "Help!"

He saw Karita spin around, alarm in her eyes. A shardling fist cracked against her shoulder, sending her tumbling. Amy and Sam were fighting with all their hearts – but no matter how many they smashed, the shardlings kept on coming.

And shardlings that had been defeated and broken to pieces were already pulling themselves back together.

It was hopeless.

The monster's mouth widened and Charlie stared into a gaping throat.

"Sali – jump for it! Save yourself!"

The stone teeth were about to snap when something zipped past Charlie's head and stabbed into one of the shardling's eyes.

An arrow! But...?

The shardling roared, dropping Charlie as it staggered backwards and burst apart.

Charlie landed on his feet, staring upwards. Sulphurous mists swirled around the upper parts of the cavern, but he could see the silhouettes of two people up at ground level.

A muscular man plunged down, crashing on to a shardling and beating it with the rim of a curiously shaped shield. The rocks burst apart, and the shardling's body crumbled. But before it even hit the ground, the man bounded on to the shoulders of a second monster, a flashing sword in his hand.

More arrows came raining down, almost too quickly for Charlie to follow. A woman stood on a finger of rock above him, firing off arrow after arrow – each one finding a perfect target in a shardling's eye.

The monsters shambled away, roaring and groaning. Sam, Karita and Amy stood back to back, shardlings all around them.

But the monsters were being repelled by the fearsome strength and amazing weapons of the warriors.

The end of a thick rope came snaking down.

"Climb!" the woman shouted.

Sam and Amy began to clamber up.

"Come!" the man shouted at Charlie in a booming voice. "Climb or die!"

Charlie ran straight for the rope and began hauling himself up, Karita just behind. Varla bounded towards the surface, vaulting from rock to rock up the sheer drop, with Wuko clinging on to her shoulders.

Charlie glanced down. The shardlings

were closing in again, but the man was fending them off, his sword slicing through solid rock, his shield hammering at their pounding fists.

Charlie came up to ground level, gasping for breath as the woman hauled him out on to solid land.

"Are you hurt?" she asked.

"I don't think so," Charlie panted, looking up into her fierce, flashing eyes.

She smiled and helped him to his feet.

The man climbed out of the chasm, his armour shining, bright sunlight glinting off the coloured jewels that studded his belt.

"Who are you guys?" gasped Sam.

Karita stepped forward, tears brimming

in her eyes. "It has been too long," she cried. "Guardians, these are the great heroes of Avantia... Elenna the Fearless and Tom, Master of Beasts!"

FOUR

Amy stared from Tom to Elenna and back again.

"Wow!" she gabbled, "You're both...it's like...I mean – *wow!*"

She had seen Tom in the magical moving pictures conjured on the wall at Karita's castle – but to have him right there in front of her was stunning.

Karita gazed into Tom's eyes, but Tom and Elenna both looked at her in confusion.

Then Elenna's face suddenly cleared. "Karita!" she gasped. "It's so good to see you!"

"You were just a girl when I last saw you, my friend," said Tom, grasping Karita's hand. "I hardly recognised you."

"And yet, you and Elenna look exactly the same," said Karita, tears in her eyes. "I have been trapped in a very strange world for almost twenty years."

"Here, it has only been three years since you went through Malvel's portal," said Tom. He turned to Amy and the others. "Who are your companions?" he asked. "They have the look of warriors, although they're only young."

"From what Karita has told us, you were about our age when you started your adventures," Charlie said mildly.

"Well said." Tom smiled. "Age is no bar to valour."

"These are the grandchildren of the Guardians who went before me through Malvel's portal," Karita explained.

"Hi," Sam said with a grin. "That's a cool shield you have there, sir."

Tom's eyebrows rose. "'Cool'?"

"He means 'amazing'," said Charlie. "He's Sam Stonewin, I'm Charlie Colton and this is Amy Errinel-Li. It's great to meet you... er...."

"Call me Tom," the grave man said with

63

a smile. He turned to Karita. "But how can they be the grandchildren of the Guardians if you have only been in their world for twenty years?"

"For me it was twenty years," said Karita. "But for the others, it was far longer. I will explain – it is a strange tale."

"Then you and Tom go and talk together," said Elenna. She looked at the cousins. "You must be hungry and thirsty after your ordeal," she said. "I have provisions in my pack. Let's move away from the chasm and rest for a while."

"Will the shardlings come after us?" asked Amy, glancing over into the great smoking cleft.

Elenna shook her head. "They won't willingly fight the Master of the Beasts."

"Or you, I'm guessing," said Amy. "You're an amazing archer."

"Thank you." Elenna smiled as she led them to a rocky knoll where they sat while she handed out bread and cheese and a flask of clear, cool water. Wuko sat on Amy's shoulder, nibbling a crust. Sali's head poked out of Charlie's shirt-front, her eyes blinking rapidly as she stared at Elenna. Spark settled on Sam's head, curling her tail around herself like a cat.

Amy noticed Elenna staring at her in curiosity as she sat beside her. "What are those devices on the sides of your head?"

Elenna asked.

Amy touched her implants. "I was born deaf," she explained. "These help me to hear."

"That is powerful magic," Elenna exclaimed. "They must be a great help to you."

"They really are," Amy agreed. "Especially when Sam talks too much – I can just switch them off!"

Charlie laughed, but Sam had a large mouthful right then, so he could only waggle his eyebrows in protest.

"I see that you are each wearing an Arcane Band," Elenna said. "I gather they were passed down from your grandparents by your mothers and fathers?"

"Kind of," said Charlie. "But it's a bit more

complicated than that. Time obviously moves differently in our world." He frowned deeply – putting on what Amy thought of as his 'calculating face'. "Hmmm. I'd like to work it out."

"Don't!" said Sam after swallowing. He looked at Elenna. "We try not to encourage Charlie when he gets started on facts and figures – he doesn't have an off switch."

Elenna stared at him. "What is an off switch?"

"It's something that would shut him up," chuckled Amy.

Sam and Charlie both laughed,

Elenna smiled widely. "It's good that you can tease each other," she said. "On a

Quest, true friendship is sometimes more important than any weapon."

"Absolutely!" Amy agreed.

"For sure!" added Sam, offering Charlie the water flask.

"I've got my own," said Charlie, pulling a water bottle out of his pocket. "It's the only thing left of everything I packed."

"I have often wondered about the realm that portal sent the Guardians to. Does your world have Beasts?" asked Elenna.

"Only the ones that came from the eggs that went through the portal," said Sam. "Like Spark, here – and Wuko and Sali."

Elenna looked at the Beasts with shining eyes. "I can sense their goodness."

"There is another one on Earth," said Amy with a shudder. "Pox – but he's not good at all."

"A corrupted Beast?" said Elenna. "How sad! What happened?"

It was a long story, and it took them a while to fill Elenna in on all the details of their encounters with Malvel and Illia Raven.

Elenna was especially thrilled by their explanation of how Malvel was banished from Earth.

"There has been no rumour of him in Avantia," she told them. "If he returned here, then he is in hiding." She shook her head. "But it's a terrible thing that his power turned the mind of a woman from your world."

"I don't think Illia's mind needed much turning," said Sam. "She's bad to the bone."

"There might be good person in her somewhere," said Amy. "If only we could find it."

"That'd be a long search!" said Charlie.

Amy nodded in agreement, but she couldn't shake the feeling that even someone as bad as Illia Raven could be reasoned with...given time.

But Pox won't let that happen. And so long as she's with him, we'll never have the chance to get through to her.

"I will miss Gustus, Fern and Dell but I'm

glad they lived long and honourable lives," said Elenna as their story came to an end. "And they would be proud to leave three noble descendants to fulfil the duties of their bloodlines."

"That's us," grinned Sam. "'Noble descendants'! I like the sound of that."

"Tom and Karita are coming," said Amy.

Tom smiled as he stood over the three Guardians.

"Welcome to Avantia, Guardians, and Beasts of the Guardians," he said solemnly. "It seems you've already won battles since you received your Arcane Bands. You do your families proud!"

"I think we'd like to do better," said Amy.

"You shall," said Tom. "I will train you as I trained your grandparents, so that you will be able to defeat any evil that threatens your world."

"Awesome!" said Sam.

Amy gazed up at Tom.

Training with the Avantian Master of Beasts... Yes, I'd say that's pretty awesome.

FIVE

Sam liked Tom and Elenna from first sight.

When I'm an adult, I want to be just like Tom – except, maybe, for the beard.

"We're heading north," said Tom as they made their way down the volcano, Karita at his side and Varla loping along in front. "To the town of Stonewin, at the mountain's foot."

"There's a town with my name, too!" said

Sam, just managing to keep up with Tom's swift strides. "Awesome!"

"Are there still Stonewins living there?" Amy asked. She and Charlie were just behind Tom, walking either side of Elenna. Wuko was gambolling among the rocks, chattering to himself.

"The Duke of Stonewin resides there," Tom replied. "He is your great-uncle." He looked into Sam's face. "You resemble him."

"I thought the same," said Elenna. "They could be brothers."

Wow! I have a duke for a great-uncle. How cool is that?

Varla paused and gave a sudden low

growl, staring at something a little way off.

Tom raised his hand for them to stop.

Sam saw movement a few yards away. Stones and rocks were gathering together, forming a shuddering pile.

"Shardling!" hissed Karita.

"Spark – go get it!" ordered Sam.

Tom touched his hand to a red jewel in his belt. "There is no need," he called to the dragon. Spark wheeled around and returned to Sam's shoulder.

"Awesome," gasped Sam, staring admiringly at Tom. "Total Master of Beasts!"

Tom strode boldly up the mountainside towards the growing heap of rocks. He stood over it for a moment, then stooped, thrusting his hand into the pile.

A moment later, he pulled his hand out and Sam saw something glowing red in his palm. Tom turned, his hand held high. Red light seeped through his fingers from a small ruby gemstone.

"This is how to destroy a shardling," he said, closing his fist.

The gem shattered. The light went out. The pile of rocks became still.

"Shardlings form around a heartstone," Tom said, walking back and displaying the crushed fragments in the palm of his hand. "Although the rocks that form the shardling are strong, the heart of the creature can be broken."

"I didn't know that," Karita said in surprise.

"The Wizard Daltec only recently discovered the weakness," explained Elenna. "Shardlings seldom come down from the mountain these days."

"I guess they know better than to mess with Tom," said Sam with a grin.

Coming around a shoulder of rock, Sam saw a town below them. It nestled between two spurs of the mountain, guarded by a tall wooden fence and with tilled fields spreading out north and west.

"That is Stonewin Town," said Tom, resting his hand on Sam's shoulder. "Home of your family."

Sam shivered with excitement as they came closer.

Soon, the high wooden gates stood open before them. People were coming and going about their daily work. They were dressed in simple clothes of wool and leather, some carrying baskets of fruit and bread, others herding cattle or geese, while still more rode horse-drawn carts laden with wheat and corn.

"Everyone looks so happy!" sighed Amy.

"The duke is a fine man," said Elenna. "The people love him."

"Good day, my lord," said a man, bowing to Sam.

"Uh...same to you," Sam replied, confused.

The man eyed Sam from head to foot as he backed away. "My lord's fashions have become very peculiar," he muttered under his breath. "Ahh, well...the youth of today!"

"I hope you are well, my lord," said a woman, curtsying before moving on.

Sam looked at Tom. "Why are they calling me 'my lord'?"

"You will see," said Tom with a smile.

They came to a stone castle that stood at the heart of the town. Elegant towers and spires rose into the blue sky and golden pennants flew in the breeze.

In the courtyard, a young man stood

beside a horse, speaking with some finely dressed courtiers.

"Duke Stonewin," called Tom, raising his hand in salute. "We wish to speak with you."

"Always at your service, Master of Beasts," said the young man, turning.

His eyes widened as he saw Sam.

He looks exactly like me, just...a year or two older!

"What magic is this?" asked the duke, staring at Sam.

"This is Sam Stonewin," Tom said quickly. "The grandson of your brother, Gustus. He has come through a portal from another world. Evil has infected his homeland and

he seeks our aid."

"Then he shall have it," cried the young duke, rushing forwards and throwing his arms around Sam in a tight embrace. "You are thrice welcome!" he cried.

Sam squirmed for a moment, embarrassed by this unexpected show of affection. But then he grinned and returned the hug.

After all, he's family, I guess.

The duke broke away and stared at Tom. "But Gustus was only a year older than me when he passed through the portal of no return. How...?"

"Time moves strangely between the realms," Tom said.

The duke nodded, then his eyes rose to Spark, still perched on Sam's head. "A beautiful Beast," he said. "Recently hatched, I think. How big will she grow?"

"In time, very big," Karita replied.

"Really?" said Sam in surprise. "Awesome!"

Maybe I'll be able to ride her. How cool will that be?

"Come inside," urged the duke. "You shall have quarters in the Tower of the West Wind. It is a suite of rooms kept only for our most revered guests."

"I like the sound of that," said Amy.

They followed the duke into a great hallway hung with colourful banners and shining armour. He led them up a wide stairway and along a corridor lined with tapestries depicting Beasts and battles and sun-kissed mountains.

Sam drank it all in, his heart pounding with excitement.

This is turning out to be even better than I imagined!

SIX

"Throw your axe, Charlie!'

Tom's voice boomed from the battlements as the huge phoenix swooped – all hooked beak and rushing claws – its blazing eyes shooting fireballs.

Charlie swung his axe with both hands, but the attacking Beast twisted in the air and soared upwards again.

"It doesn't work like that!" Charlie shouted, stumbling backwards.

The axe is part of the band – I can't just chuck it at things.

The training wasn't going well. Every time Charlie and his cousins thought they had the phoenix trapped in the courtyard, it would drive them back with a volley of fireballs from its blazing eyes, and its great wings would lift it far above their heads.

It was so quick in the air that even Sam, throwing his hook and chain with all his strength, was unable to grapple it. Amy had been amazing, using her mace like a baseball bat, fending off fireballs and sending them spinning in all directions.

"Trust yourself!" Tom urged.

This is never going to work.

Charlie spread his feet, balancing himself. He shoved aside his fear, snapped his right arm forwards and let the weapon fly. To his amazement it slid free of the band and cartwheeled though the air.

It worked!

The weapon ruffled the Beast's wing-feathers as it skimmed past.

Rats! Missed!

"Not bad, Charlie!" Sam yelled.

The phoenix lowered its head, staring at Charlie, its eyes beginning to glow.

Uh-oh! Fireballs.

And now Charlie had no axe to defend himself.

But at the apex of its flight, the axe spun

in a tight loop and came plunging back towards Charlie's outstretched hand.

The hilt slammed into his fingers and he grabbed hold of it.

"Wow!" he gasped, almost knocked off his feet by the impact. "It comes back!"

There was a smattering of applause from the watchers on the battlements.

"Well done, Charlie!" cried Karita.

"You have powers greater than you thought!" shouted Elenna. "You all do!"

The Beast was hovering above the palace; at any moment, deadly fireballs would stream from its eyes.

"The Beast's advantage is flight," boomed Tom. "Sam – what must you do next?"

"Bring it down," shouted Sam. "But how?"

"Do not swing your weapon around your head," Tom called down. "Launch it from your Arcane Band."

Sam gripped the hook in his hand. "Here goes nothing!"

He thrust his arm out, letting out a whoop of surprise as the hook sped into the air faster than an arrow, the chain reeling out beyond. "It's never gone that far before!" he yelled.

"Or that fast!" added Amy.

The hook rose above the phoenix. Sam gave an expert flick of the chain and the hook wheeled around, circling the Beast's body and snapping on to the chain under its belly.

"Just like a lasso!" Sam yelled. "Yee-*hah!*" He tugged on the chain and it came reeling in, dragging the phoenix down.

But the Beast was far from beaten. As it dropped out of the sky, fireballs rained down on to the Guardians.

"Amy – your shield!" Tom shouted.

Instantly, Amy's spiked mace morphed into a round shield. She held it up as fireballs pelted down all around her.

But the ones that struck her shield bounced back, blazing up into the sky like rockets, hurtling into the Beast's body, setting the feathers alight.

The phoenix burst into flames and vanished, leaving only a puff of reddish cloud.

Tom spread his arms, a wide smile on his face. "Victory!" he shouted. "The Beast is no more. The test is over."

Sam leaped up, punching the air with his fist. "In your face, Beast!" he hollered. "No one messes with the Guardians."

"Calm yourself," Karita called down with a laugh. "It was only an illusion conjured by the apprentice Wizard, Callard – a real Beast will not be so easily defeated."

Charlie, Amy and Sam gathered together under the battlements.

"I never knew my shield could reflect

fireballs," Amy said, her eyes shining. "And you and your axe, Charlie – that was so cool."

"We're invincible," exclaimed Sam.

"You are all more skilled than you know," said Elenna, as she and the others made their way down the stone stairway to the courtyard.

Tom grasped each of the cousins by the hand. "Well done, Amy. Well done, Charlie. Well done, Sam!"

Karita smiled. "I am prouder of you than I can say," she told them. "You have come a long way since first we met."

"We couldn't have done it without you," Amy said, echoing exactly what Charlie was thinking.

"Excuse me," he said. "I was just wondering...are there other things our Arcane Bands can do?"

"One step at a time, Charlie," said Tom. "Learn to use your new-found skills in a real battle before you go looking for more."

It had been two days since they had arrived through the portal, and every spare moment had been spent sparring with Tom, Elenna and Karita in the Duke of Stonewin's castle. The young duke had spent a lot of time with them, and genuine friendships had developed.

There's a real bond between Sam and the duke – after they went on that tour of the castle together, Sam couldn't stop talking about him.

Charlie had also noticed how often Karita and Elenna spent time speaking quietly. He knew Karita missed her homeland –it must have been nice for her to have a fellow Avantian to chat with.

Charlie knew he should be feeling exhausted and sore after all those hours of hard work, but instead he felt full of life and energy.

Maybe it's the air in Avantia? After all, we are one quarter Avantian.

"I believe you have learned enough to return to your own world," Tom said. "You have the skills now to face Earth's worst villains without fear."

"Uhm, excuse me," Charlie said raising his arm. "I've been thinking about the way time works here and on Earth. We've been in Avantia about two and a half days so far – which must be a whole lot longer on Earth!" He looked from Amy to Sam. "Our parents will be going crazy!"

Amy's hands flew to her face. "I never thought of that!" she gasped, while Sam stared at Charlie with horrified eyes.

"Have no fear," said the duke. "I have spoken about this with Callard, and he tells me the artefact you used to get here will return you to your own world only moments after you left."

"And now it is time for you to depart,"

said Tom, putting a hand into his tunic pocket and drawing something out. "I have a gift for you."

He opened his hand. A smooth round stone lay in his palm, milky white with threads of coral running through it. "This is a Tonguestone," he explained. "Should you ever be in dire peril, hold it to your forehead and speak the words: 'Tom, Master of Beasts, we are in need'. I will hear you, and give you what advice I can."

He handed the stone to Charlie. It felt warm against his skin.

"Keep it safe," warned Elenna. "It may save you if the danger is too great."

"I will!" said Charlie, slipping the

Tonguestone into his pocket.

"And now it is time for us to return," said Karita, Varla gliding to stand at her side. She took out the compass and Charlie, Sam and Amy gathered around her. Wuko jumped on to Amy's shoulder, Sali slipped into Charlie's shirt-front and Spark perched on Sam's head.

Charlie felt torn – Avantia had begun to feel like a second home, and he would have loved to spend more time exploring this strange and fantastic new world.

But Illia Raven needs to be dealt with – and we're the only ones who can do that.

He sighed as he raised his arm. The Arcane Band glowed.

"Farewell, Guardians!" called Tom as he and Elenna and the duke backed away.

"Bye," called Sam. "It's been a blast!"

"I hope we'll see you again some day," Amy added.

"Some day soon," Charlie put in.

"All things are possible." Elenna's voice faded as Karita activated the compass and a fire-rimmed portal opened in the air.

"We are heading for Dubai," Karita told the Guardians. "We know that's where Illia is, and doubtless the Beast is with her – so be wary!"

Charlie and the others jumped into the black hole and the land of Avantia vanished in a fiery haze.

SEVEN

Amy shielded her eyes against a blaze of sunlight as the portal vanished at their backs.

The walls of a massive building curved out over them, faced with mirrored windows that dazzlingly reflected sea and sky. Ahead, beyond a road that shimmered in the heat, a long beach led to lapping waters, the golden sand lined with deckchairs under white umbrellas. Palm trees swayed in a gentle, hot breeze. There were plenty of people coming and going, some dressed in traditional Arabic clothing and others in the shorts and T-shirts of tourists.

Amy turned and saw a stunning skyline of tall, slender office blocks, and ultra-modern towers stretching away inland.

"This building is Obsidian Corp's newest research centre," said Karita. "Illia is inside. Varla will explore and seek out a safe way into the building."

The Stealth Panther slipped away like a shadow: one moment, Amy could see her clearly; the next, she was gone.

"Spark can help," Sam said. He lifted his hand to his head and the little dragon

stepped from his cap on to his wrist. "Keep a low profile," Sam explained. "Fly up and see if you can spot Illia, or Pox."

Spark opened her wings and sped upwards, keeping close to the building, dwindling away until she was just a speck against the sky.

By her side, Amy noticed Charlie looking thoughtful.

"What's wrong?" she asked him.

"Nothing," he said. Then he grinned, beckoning her away from Karita and Sam. "I just worked it out," he whispered. "The Duke of Stonewin was Sam's grandfather's younger brother, right?"

"Yes."

"So, Sam's grandfather would have become the duke if he hadn't gone through the portal." Charlie gave her a mischievous look. "Which means that Sam's *dad* would have been next in line..."

Amy realised what Charlie was hinting at. "Sam's the rightful Duke of Stonewin," she breathed, glancing at their friend. "We can't tell him! His head's big enough already!"

Charlie nodded. "He'd insist we call him 'Duke Sam.'"

They both spluttered with laughter.

"What's the gag?" Sam asked, staring over at them.

"Nothing at all, Your Majesty," giggled Amy.

Sam looked blankly at her. "Huh?"

"The Beasts return," said Karita. Varla appeared at her side, her fur glowing like blue velvet, her eyes darkly reflecting the sky.

Spark sped down, landing on Sam's outstretched wrist and giving out a series of sharp cries.

"Spark says the place is full of people," Sam translated. "It's like a regular office block, except for the laboratories at the very top."

"Did she sense the presence of a Beast?" asked Karita.

"Not for certain," Sam said. "But there's definitely something nasty up there."

"Varla has discovered a way to get inside without being seen," said Karita. "Follow close."

They moved around to the back of the building. Amy noticed Charlie now had *two* bulges under his shirt.

"It's a water bottle," he explained. "If we get into a fight Sali will be able to help out."

Amy nodded. Sali was small and not very strong, but her magical ability to dive into one pool of water and instantly reappear from another was great for distracting and confusing enemies. And Amy had the uneasy feeling they would need all the tactics they could muster if they were to defeat Illia and that horrible Beast of hers.

Varla led them to a service entrance; a wide shutter at the end of a tunnel that dived under the back of the building.

Karita pointed to a grey metal box set high on the wall. "That's the alarm system," she said. "Wuko needs to disable it."

"Go for it, boy," urged Amy. With a grin, Wuko leaped from her shoulder and swarmed up the wall to the box. He spread one hand out on the metal cover.

His hand glowed and there was a hiss from the box. Wuko smiled down at Amy.

"Good boy!" she called, opening her arms as he jumped down.

"And now the shutter," Karita said.

"Do your thing, Spark," said Sam.

Spark swooped and ran a burst of bright flame along the bottom of the shutter. Soon, growing droplets of melted metal started to drip from it. Sam easily pulled the shutter upwards and went inside with Charlie, Amy, Karita, and Varla following close behind.

They entered a long concrete area with a ceiling held up by thick, square pillars.

"There's a lift," said Amy, pointing across the room.

"Elevators will have surveillance cameras," said Sam. "Stairs would be safer."

Charlie looked at him in dismay. "That lift shows sixty-three floors," he groaned. "And Spark said the laboratories are right at the top."

Karita gave a wry smile. "Then it is good you've been training," she said, heading for doors that showed a staircase sign.

It took them some time to climb to the top of the building. Varla went ahead to warn them of any Obsidian Corp employees using the stairs above them.

Amy noticed Charlie puffing and blowing as they approached the upper levels of the building, and even she felt the strain in her thighs and shins.

They finally came to a landing with a sign by the doors: *LabTech Level Alpha*.

"We start here," Karita whispered, showing no sign of weariness after the long climb. "Stealth is vital – if we are to stand any chance of vanquishing Illia and her Beast, we must take them by surprise."

The plan was to attack as a team, targeting Pox first. Amy couldn't help shivering at the thought of the hideous skeletal bird, its body rimmed with green fire, its eyes like pools of burning poison.

Wuko tightened his arms around her neck and nuzzled against her. As she stroked him, new courage flowed through her veins. "Thanks, Wuko," she whispered, her heart swelling with love for the Beast. "That makes me feel much better."

They passed through the doors and into a long, curving corridor studded to either side with glass-panelled doors.

"Deffo laboratories," murmured Charlie.

Suddenly, a door opened and a man in a white coat stepped into their path.

Karita lifted her hand in warning and they stopped dead. Amy's heart leaped in alarm.

We're done for.

But the man glided past them, his pale face strangely blank, his eyes filled with an eerie green light.

Sam stared after the man as he passed through another doorway. "What the heck was that?" he gasped. "It was like he didn't even see us."

Another door opened, and two women

entered the corridor. They had the same pale, blank faces, and their eyes glowed green. They passed the Guardians, staring straight ahead, their movements oddly stiff and jerky.

"Did you see the green fire in their eyes?" said Karita. "They are in Pox's thrall."

"They're like zombies!" murmured Charlie. "So creepy!"

"It will work to our advantage, I think," said Karita. "If all the people here are under the same spell, they may ignore us."

"But how do we help them?" Amy asked.

"Stopping Pox is the only way," Karita said grimly. Amy knew she was right, but she couldn't help wondering what other evils the corrupted Beast was capable of.

They continued along the corridor, noticing people inside the laboratories, all pale and stiff, and empty-faced as they went about their work.

Another man approached around the bend of the corridor and Amy recoiled as he almost walked straight into her.

Sam approached the man and waved his hand in his face.

"Sam, don't!" hissed Karita.

"This is so weird," Sam said. "You could set off a firecracker under his nose and he wouldn't even – ahh!"

The man's hand jerked up, his fingers closing around Sam's arm. The green eyes stared at Sam's Arcane Band.

"Interloper!" the man snarled, baring his teeth. "You must die!"

Sam managed to wrest his arm free, backing away as Spark leaped into the air, breathing fire.

"No, Spark," Sam cried. "Don't hurt him – he can't help himself!"

The zombie-man tilted his head back and let out a chilling, inhuman roar. Instinctively, Amy adjusted her hearing implant to a lower setting and the noise lessened.

Moments later, doors burst open all along the corridor and more zombies tumbled out, arms outstretched towards the Guardians.

"Run!" cried Karita, pointing to a set of

doors that led to another stairway. "Head upwards – find Illia Raven and her Beast. Varla and I will draw these poor creatures away if we can."

The three cousins flung themselves at the doors and burst through. They held the doors closed as the zombies beat on them, growling and snarling.

"Look what you did!" gasped Charlie, glaring at Sam, his shoulder to the doors. "You woke them all up!"

"How was I to know?" yelled Sam.

Amy had her back to the doors, her leg muscles strained and aching from the long climb, digging her heels in as she felt the zombies thumping and punching to get

through to them.

"If zombies eat brains like in the movies," panted Charlie, "Sam's got nothing to lose!"

"Hey!" Sam shouted.

The doors shook as the zombies pounded them, each blow adding to the pain in Amy's body.

How...much...longer...?

All the lights went out in an instant, plunging the stairwell into terrifying darkness.

"That's all we need!" came Sam's voice.

A phone light flashed on, and then a second. Charlie and Sam aimed the beams up the stairs ahead.

"We can't keep them from breaking

through," Charlie shouted. "We've got to run for it!"

Amy threw herself away from the doors and followed Charlie and Sam as they raced up the stairs. Behind them, the doors burst open and the zombies tumbled through, roaring and clawing at the air.

"Uh-oh!" Sam was a few steps ahead of Amy and Charlie, his phone-light skittering up the stairs. "Really, really not good!"

Amy stared up. Another group of zombies were clambering awkwardly down the stairs, towards them.

Wuko growled, his eyes shining.

"No, we mustn't hurt them," Amy explained. "They can't help themselves."

The zombies shambled closer, climbing up from below and lumbering down from above.

"I don't suppose we can talk this over?" called Sam, flashing his phone-light into the eyes of the leading zombies.

All the zombies roared at once – a terrifying noise that froze Amy's blood.

"I didn't think so," said Sam.

The zombies closed in, snarling and reaching out with clutching fingers.

Amy struggled as several pairs of cold hands caught hold of her. All she could see were wild green-flecked eyes and gnashing teeth.

Then she heard a whirring from above. A

dark figure came gliding down the stairwell on a slender rope.

There was a bright flash as some kind of weapon was discharged. The zombies tumbled back, howling and shrieking. Some fell, and others tripped over them.

The dark figure vaulted the banister, unhitched the rope and landed on the stairs, firing the stun gun in all directions. Their rescuer was dressed all in black, with a ski mask and night-vision goggles obscuring their face.

"Follow me," called a muffled voice, as the black-clad warrior bounded down the steps, knocking zombies to either side and still firing its weapon.

Amy and the boys exchanged a quick look, then chased after the figure.

Who is that?

When they reached for a landing, the lithe figure dived through the doors, leading them along a lightless corridor and into another room. They gasped for breath as the dark figure slammed and locked the door.

"Thanks!" panted Sam. "Another couple of seconds and we'd have been zombie-food for sure!" He glanced at Charlie. "Brains or no brains!"

Their rescuer stood against the door, the stun-gun hanging from a cord around their neck.

"Who are you?" asked Amy, switching her implants to a higher setting now that the noise of battle had died down.

The figure lifted a hand to its chin and pulled off the ski mask and goggles to reveal the sharp face and dishevelled hair of Illia Raven.

"I'm in big trouble here," the woman gasped. "And if you don't help me, we're all going to die!"

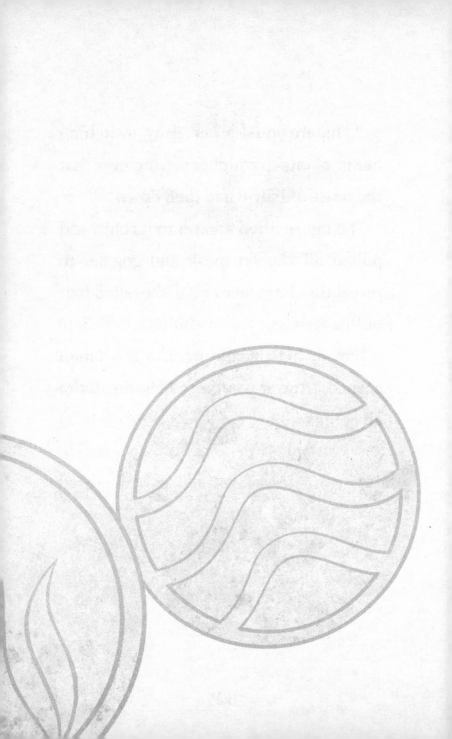

EIGHT

"You have *got* to be kidding me!" Sam yelled. He launched his hook and chain, taking Illia's feet out from under her.

Amy and Charlie sprang forwards and, in a moment, both mace and axe were poised above the fallen woman's head.

She lifted her hands pleadingly. "You have to trust me," she cried.

"We really *don't*!" said Charlie.

Illia took a shuddering breath. "If you don't help me stop Pox, he'll destroy the whole world," she said, her voice trembling. "He's become a monster!"

"He's *become* a monster?" Sam echoed. "Lady, he was a monster from the moment you hatched him."

"And it didn't seem to bother you then," added Charlie.

Amy stooped, peering into Illia's eyes. "You've got thirty seconds," she said. "Convince us this isn't a trick."

Illia sat up, her chest heaving. She pointed to the door. "Those guys out there," she began. "That's how we'll all look if we don't stop Pox. He consumes a part of your life energy and gets in your brain." She grimaced. "If I hadn't come up with a blocking device, I'd already be one of them."

"She's faking it," said Sam. "This is totally a trap."

"I'm not so sure," said Amy. She looked carefully into Illia's frightened face. "I think she's telling the truth."

"You *trust* her?" gasped Charlie.

"No, but I think she's scared." Amy stared down at Illia. "You bit off more than you could chew when you hatched that thing, didn't you?"

"That's exactly what I did," Illia replied. "Now, are you Guardians going to do your jobs and help me stop Pox, or are you OK with him wrecking this entire planet?"

Sam eyed her dubiously.

Can we really trust her, or is this just a sneaky scheme to zombify us all?

"Group huddle," Sam said. "Spark, Wuko, Sali – keep an eye on Illia. If she makes a move, take her down!"

Sam, Amy and Charlie drew away to the other end of the room.

"Vote?" suggested Charlie. "Those who think we should help her?"

Amy put her hand up. Charlie hesitated, then voted 'yes'. They both looked at Sam.

He sighed. "This could be the dumbest thing we've ever done," he said, reluctantly raising his hand.

They went back to Illia and Amy helped her to her feet. When they unlocked the door to the room, there was no sign of the zombies.

"Why did all the lights go out?" asked Charlie.

"I cut the power when I saw you were under attack," Illia said, pointing to a CCTV camera high on the wall. "I thought you'd do better in the dark."

"So are you taking us to Pox?" asked Sam.

"Eventually," Illia replied.

"What does *that* mean?" asked Charlie.

"Pox isn't here at the lab any more," Illia explained. "After he turned all my staff into..." She paused.

"Zombies?" offered Charlie.

She frowned then shrugged. "After that, he burst through the roof and flew into the desert. I'm taking you up to the helicopter to track him."

Amy took out her phone. "I'm calling Karita to let her know everything's OK."

As Amy pressed Karita's number, they followed Illia through a set of double doors into a soft glow of dusky light that poured through floor-to-ceiling windows.

Wow! It's evening already – I totally lost track of time in there.

Ahead of them, a spiral staircase wound up to a high landing.

"Karita, are you OK?" Amy said into the

phone. She listened, then turned to the others. "She and Varla are keeping the zombies busy."

As they climbed the stairs, Amy filled Karita in on what had happened.

"Yes, I think we can trust her," Amy said. "For now."

"Tell her you can trust me full stop," insisted Illia. "I'm done with Beasts and magic."

"And what about ruling the world?" Sam asked dryly. "Are you done with that, too?"

"Yes," Illia responded flatly. "I'm finished with all of it. Once Pox has been dealt with, I'll never cause trouble again – and that's a promise!"

She opened a metal door at the top of the staircase and they stepped out on to the flat roof. After the cool confines of the air-conditioned building, the heat hit them like a wall. The sky was darkening from the west, where a few early stars already glimmered.

"Yes, we'll be careful," Amy said into her phone. "You, too." She slipped it into her pocket. "Karita says, good luck."

A black helicopter was waiting on the helipad. The three Guardians and their Beasts followed Illia across the pad and into the aircraft.

Illia got into the pilot's seat. "Strap yourselves in," she called over her shoulder as she switched the motor on. The rotor blades began turning, with a low *whump-whump-whump* sound.

The three cousins found themselves seats and belted up. Spark nestled on Sam's shoulder and Wuko settled down into Amy's lap. As usual, Sali slipped inside Charlie's shirt.

As they sped along, the futuristic cityscape of Dubai slid away beneath them, its thousands of lights shining out as the sky darkened. Soon, they were out over a flat, sun-baked landscape.

They passed over a few lit-up towns and settlements threaded together by narrow roads; then they came into the open desert, mile after mile of empty wasteland stretching away in all directions.

Sam heard Illia speaking to herself. "What on earth is that?"

The helicopter swerved, as she changed course.

Something's wrong.

Illia called to them. "Do you see that light on the horizon?"

They stared through the window.

"I see it," said Charlie, narrowing his eyes. "It's sort of...green?"

"And it's getting bigger," said Sam in sudden alarm.

To the east, the green cloud was rushing forwards – and at its heart was a horribly

familiar shape.

"Pox!" gasped Amy. "And look at the size of him now!"

Sam groaned. *He's gotten as big as a fighter jet! Illia sure didn't warn us about that.*

The evil Beast soared towards them through the sky, green flames spinning out from his massive body, his silhouette blotting out the stars.

Sam's heart thundered as he saw the monstrous bird closing in at terrifying speed, his eyes gleaming with malice.

"Hold tight!" yelled Illia. She wrestled with the controls and the helicopter nose-dived under the Beast.

But one of Pox's claws raked along the spine of the helicopter, ripping off the tail rotor. Illia let out a yell of alarm as the aircraft went into a spin and spiralled downwards.

Hanging by his seatbelt, Sam saw the ground rushing up to hit them. He pulled Spark down off his shoulder and cradled her in his arms.

Kerrrwhuuumph!

The helicopter smacked into the ground with bone-shaking force.

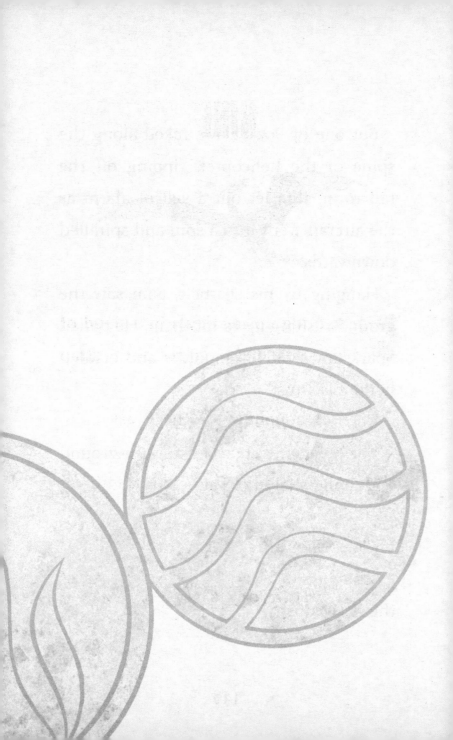

NINE

Charlie hung upside down in a cloud of choking dust, held in place by the strap of his seatbelt.

His first thought was for his Beast.

Sali?

He felt her paddling at his chest with her six little feet.

Phew! She's alive.

"You guys OK?" Sam's voice came out of the fog of dust.

"I'm fine." Amy's voice sounded strained. She called out. "Illia?"

There was no response from the cockpit of the helicopter.

Charlie heard a slither and a thud. A moment later, Sam was helping him out of his seatbelt. It was awkward to turn over while hanging upside down, but Sam kept a firm hold on him. They quickly rescued Amy.

"Get out," Sam told them. "The fuel tank might explode. I'll check on Illia."

"We're not leaving without you," said Charlie.

They fumbled through the fog to the front of the helicopter. Illia had fallen out of her seat. She wasn't moving.

They dragged her out and laid her in the sand.

Amy knelt over her. "She's out cold."

Sam stared up at the evening sky. "Where's Pox gone?" he asked.

"Maybe he thinks he's killed us," Charlie said, peering into the distance.

"Let's hope so," said Amy.

Sam clambered up on to the inverted helicopter and scanned the horizon in every direction. "I see something!" he called, pointing. "A green dome, not far off. No way is it natural."

"Is it Pox's lair?" Charlie asked.

"What else?" Sam slithered down. "So –

are we going to finish this?"

Amy looked at Illia. "We'll leave her in the recovery position," she said. "Hopefully she'll be OK." She turned to Wuko, who was swinging on one of the bent and broken rotor blades. "Come here, Wuko," she called. "This is quiet time, OK? We need to sneak up on that bad Beast."

Wuko nodded and leaped into Amy's arms.

Spark settled on Sam's shoulder as the three Guardians set off across the twilight desert.

They quickly discovered it wasn't quite as featureless as they had thought. The sun-baked ground was ridged with steep, rocky outcrops.

Soon, Charlie was feeling the heat and the discomfort of the long hike.

I could do with a drink. But we might need the water so Sali can join in the fight.

Gradually, the green dome drew closer, and at last, they climbed up to a sharp rim and found themselves staring down at the uncanny formation.

It was constructed of spiked and razor-edged glass, a deep and sinister green colour that pulsed and rippled in a way that reminded Charlie of the egg from which the Beast had been hatched.

"Keep low," murmured Sam. "If he sees us coming, we're toast." He slithered down the far side of the hill with Amy and Charlie right behind.

Charlie expected the huge shape of Pox to suddenly swoop out of nowhere, firing hoops of green fire at them. But nothing happened as they crept slowly closer to the huge glass dome.

Pox must have made this by melting sand. How powerful is he now?

"How do we get inside?" whispered Amy.

Sam pointed to a dark nook at the base of the dome away to their left.

The shadow was a low opening. Stalagmites and stalactites of sharp glass jutted up and down, so that the entrance looked like an open mouth waiting for the

chance to snap shut on them.

And rip us to tiny pieces! No – don't think stuff like that, Charlie.

"I can't hear anything," said Sam as they came to the edge of the entryway.

"I've put my implants on their highest setting," Amy said. "Let me listen."

She slipped under the fanged gape of the opening, stooping low, becoming still. A few moments later, she came back out.

"He's definitely in there," she said. "Do we have a plan?"

"We have to keep him contained," Sam said. "That's our only chance." He turned to Spark. "I need a supernova, girl," he told her. "Melt the glass above the entrance so it forms a wall to stop Pox getting out. Got it?"

Spark snorted and butted Sam's forehead.

Sam grinned. "I think that's a 'yes'," he said. "As for the rest of us – we just give it all we've got, right?" His eyes gleamed. "This is what we've been training for. This is why we were given the Arcane Bands."

"While there's breath in our lungs, we'll fight," said Amy, her voice grim and determined.

"Three Guardians and three Beasts," said Charlie. "Pox doesn't stand a chance!"

Fake it till you make it, as my granddad used to say!

"Let's roll!" growled Sam.

They headed under the sharp-toothed entrance and entered a world of gloomy green shadows. It gave Charlie the feeling he was deep underwater. The air was hot and stifling and the whole place stank.

Pox was on the ground, wings folded, his bent back towards them. His head was lowered, and Charlie heard tearing and chomping sounds.

I don't even want to think what it's eating!

The evil Beast was more hideous than ever as he loomed over them, his skeletal body lapped with billowing green flame, the feathers of his wings and tail rank and scabbed.

Sam gestured for Charlie to go right and Amy to go left.

They would attack from all sides at once.

As Charlie crept around the Beast, he saw that Pox was pecking at the carcass of some poor animal. It might have been a cow or a horse – there was so little of it left, it was hard to tell.

Charlie concentrated, and a moment later, his axe was in his fist. In his other hand, he held the water bottle, lid off and ready.

There was a clattering sound as Sam's hook and chain spun out, sweeping around the Beast's skeletal legs.

"*Krawwwwkkkkk!*"

Pox let out a cry of anger and surprise as Sam yanked on the chain. The Beast's wings opened, and he rose into the air. Wuko leaped from Amy's arms and landed high on Pox's back, pressing glowing hands on to the Beast's skull.

Green light sprayed out of Wuko's eyes, and Charlie saw the flames that surrounded the phoenix waver and flicker.

Behind him, he heard a sound like a blowtorch. Spark was zipping back and forth across the entrance, shooting a fierce blue fire at the glass – and already, great molten blobs of it were dripping down, forming a barrier of thick glass bars.

Pox rose into the air, screaming in rage

and aiming hoops of sorcerous green fire at Sam. Sam crouched low, bathed in flames. He dug his heels in to stop being dragged off his feet, yanking his chain with all his might to try and drag Pox down.

Charlie flung his axe. It cracked into Pox's head, snapping his neck sideways. The axe came whirring back to Charlie's grip, but the Beast's head turned, and aimed deadly fire.

Sam was impervious to flame, so he could survive such an attack – but Charlie had no such defences. He dived aside as a wave of fire drilled into the ground, spitting gobs of molten glass. The flames licked closer as Charlie struggled to scramble free.

But then Amy was standing over him, her shield held high, deflecting the blast of green flame back towards Pox, striking his head and sending the great Beast reeling back.

Pox's wing swung down, hitting Amy and flinging her across the dome.

Sam jerked his chain from side to side to keep the Beast unbalanced.

Shaking his head, Pox towered over Charlie, opening his beak. Flames flickered in his throat. Charlie spilled water on to the ground and Sali leaped out of his shirt-front and dived in.

Charlie got to his feet and squeezed the bottle. A jet of water sprayed into Pox's face. Sali appeared from the water, six legs extended, six-fingered feet splayed out as she slammed into the Beast's eye.

Shrieking in pain, Pox dropped out of the air, the fires of his body almost extinguished by Wuko. But the impact jarred the little Beast off Pox's back and he tumbled to the ground with a yelp.

Sam heaved on his chain, keeping the evil Beast's legs tightly bound.

Sali sailed into Charlie's arms. "That was fantastic, girl!" he gasped.

Amy was on her feet again. She rushed in fearlessly, striking Pox with her spiked mace. It ripped through the broken feathers, tearing at the thin flesh that covered his bones.

Sam unwound the chain from around the Beast's legs and pulled it in, hand over hand. Then he let it surge out again, this time coiling around Pox's neck.

The hideous Beast flapped wildly, turning and crawling towards the entrance to escape.

But Spark had done her job! Thick pillars of glass blocked the way out.

He's trapped! We've got him!

Then Pox reared up, dragging Sam off his feet.

Charlie flung his axe. The sharp blade sheared through a bone in the Beast's wing. The useless wing crumpled down – but to

Charlie's horror, he saw green fire gather at the break, and a moment later the wing was mended.

The same was true of the damage Amy's mace was doing. No matter how she hacked and chopped at the Beast's leathery flesh, the cuts healed within moments.

Even Pox's wounded eye was beginning to glow again with green fire.

Charlie remembered how they'd come close to vanquishing Pox back when they fought him in Egypt, but then he'd come back to life.

Can a phoenix even be *killed?*

But then Charlie spotted something. Amy was swinging her mace with all her might into the Beast's chest, cutting to reveal great curving rib-bones.

And somewhere inside the cavern of ribs, Charlie saw a fierce green glow.

It's like the heartstone that keeps a Shardling together!

Charlie sent a quick thought to Sali as he spilled more water on the ground.

Sali plunged in. Charlie ran in past Amy, aiming the bottle high and squeezing. The last of the water spurted up and, an instant later, Sali emerged, leaping in through one of the cuts Amy had made to snatch the heartstone, and wheel away with it in her arms.

Screaming, Pox stabbed at her with his

beak, knocking the heartstone from her grasp and sending her spinning.

"Sali! No!"

Sam came bounding over Pox's shoulder, the hook and chain rocketing out from his wrist.

Pox reared back, the green light in his eyes wavering.

A moment later, Sam's hook stabbed into the falling heartstone.

Pox's scream faded to a wail as the green fires died. He collapsed into a rubble of bones and feathers.

"We did it!" yelled Amy as Sam reeled the hook in and grabbed the green stone, holding it in the air in triumph.

"Way to go, team!" he shouted.

But Charlie saw green fire spilling from between Sam's fingers.

"Watch out!" he shouted.

Tendrils of green fire spun out from the heartstone, flickering over the Beast's bones. They began to twitch and move and slide together.

Pox was regenerating again! Even stabbing the Beast in the heart wasn't enough!

"Spark!" howled Sam. "Flame on!"

He held the heartstone at arm's length as Spark zoomed in.

Amy and Charlie stumbled back as the little dragon hovered over Sam, searing the heartstone with blue fire.

Charlie could see that even Sam found the heat brutal. Anyone else would have been a human torch by now.

All the while, Pox's body was gathering, bones knitting to bones, feathers re-attaching themselves, the skull lifting as the monstrous green light began to glow again in its eyes.

Charlie's bottle was empty, but he saw Sali bounce towards the Beast's head. She opened her wide mouth and a jet of water sprayed out, dousing the fire that was growing in its eyes.

Wow! I didn't know she could do that!

Charlie dashed in, hacking at the bones,

Amy at his side, wielding her mace. A claw grabbed Charlie's legs, digging in painfully.

Despite all their efforts, Pox was regenerating faster than they could break the bones apart.

"Gotcha!" Sam's voice rang out above the other noise.

The claw broke apart around Charlie's legs. Pox's great head crashed down, the neck-bones splintering.

Gasping and exhausted, Charlie looked to where Sam was standing with green dust falling from his fingers.

The heartstone had burned away to nothing.

And as Charlie looked, the bones and feathers of the defeated Beast crumbled to ash all around them.

Sam looked thoughtfully at his unburnt hand. "It got a bit warm there for a moment," he said with a grin. "But I think we can call that game, set and match, Guardians!"

TEN

"My head hurts," groaned Illia, leaning heavily on Amy's shoulder as they stepped out of a small pool of water.

"You deserve it, for all the things you've done recently," Amy replied.

"That's probably true," sighed Illia.

They were back in the Obsidian Corp building in Dubai. After a brief mobile phone conversation with Amy, Karita had spilled a pool of water there so that Sali could portal Illia and the Guardians back to the city.

Sam, Spark, Wuko and Charlie were already waiting for them, along with Karita and Varla. It was night now, and the city burned with thousands of lights.

The Shadow Panther growled and sharpened her claws on the floor when she saw Illia Raven. Karita glowered at the villain, her knuckles white as she gripped her bo-staff.

Illia dropped to her knees in front of Karita, her head bowed. "I'm ready to take my punishment," she said. "I make no excuses for my actions."

Karita stared at her, but Amy couldn't

make out what the Avantian woman was thinking.

"Some might say you deserve death..." Karita began.

"No!" cried Amy, stepping between them. "She's genuinely sorry."

"And we wouldn't have defeated Pox without her help," added Charlie.

Karita smiled grimly. "As I was about to say," she began, "*some* might say you deserve death, but I believe you deserve a second chance, Illia Raven." Her eyes blazed. "Will you use this chance for good?"

"I will," said Illia.

"Then all is well." Karita rested her bo-staff on her shoulder. "When the Beast died, the spell that had held your people in thrall was broken. They seem to have regained their health as well. They are gathered in one of the conference rooms downstairs. You should go to them and give them new orders." She frowned. "And this time, make sure that Obsidian Corp works for the *benefit* of humankind, not for its destruction."

"I will," said Illia, standing up. "That's a promise."

"Go!" commanded Karita.

Illia walked unsteadily away down the corridor.

"Has she really learned her lesson?" wondered Sam.

"I think so," said Amy.

"I hope so," added Charlie.

"As do we all," said Karita. "But you Guardians should keep one eye on her, to be on the safe side." She looked at Sali. "Will you take us home, good Beast?"

Sali leaped from Charlie's arms. The puddle of water gleamed to reveal the towers and parapets of Karita's castle.

"Home!" echoed Amy as they stepped one by one into the rippling pool.

"Adventures are fine," said Sam as they all stood in the forecourt of Karita's castle. "But it's good to be back in the UK."

"It really is," added Amy, gazing around fondly at the familiar woodlands and an evening sky dotted with stars. "Home sweet home."

"Home indeed, for my Guardian friends," said Karita.

"Sorry," said Amy. "I forgot – Avantia is really your home."

"Indeed," said Karita with a sad smile. "But I meant this is to be your home – this castle."

"Huh?" said Sam.

"Excuse me?" said Charlie.

"What do you mean?" asked Amy, very puzzled.

"I am giving this castle and the lands

that surround it to the three of you, to keep for your own," Karita explained. "There is money put aside for its upkeep for many years to come. The documents are already written and signed, and are safe with my solicitor." She smiled widely. "She will be in contact with you in good time."

"We're getting the castle?" breathed Charlie. "But...but...*why?*"

"I think I know why," said Amy, her heart aching as she looked at Karita. "You're going home to Avantia, aren't you?"

"I am," said Karita. "My task was to train you so that you could keep your world safe."

"But we need more training!" exclaimed Sam.

Karita shook her head. "You don't," she said. "Work together, learn the secrets of your Arcane Bands. You can do it without me."

"She's right," said Amy. She gave Karita a rueful smile. "You deserve to go home."

"You have the Tonguestone that Tom gave you," said Karita. "This is not goodbye for ever – we shall meet again, I am sure, and if ever you feel overmatched, make contact with Avantia and help will come to you." She moved among them, resting her hand on each of their shoulders while Varla prowled at her side.

It was sad to say goodbye, but Amy and the others knew how much Karita missed her home realm.

Using the compass, they opened a portal to Avantia. After warm embraces and some hearty licks from Varla, Karita stepped through with her loyal Stealth Panther at her side.

Amy caught a fleeting glimpse of Tom and Elenna standing at the open doorway of Stonewin Castle. Smiling, the two heroes of Avantia opened their arms as Karita and Varla ran forward.

They must have known somehow that she was coming!

The portal closed with a soft fizzing sound.

Amy turned to the others, tears pricking

at her eyes. "Group hug?" she asked her cousins, her voice croaky.

Sam, Charlie and Amy gathered together, their arms tight around one another, their heads lowered. Amy felt bathed in Wuko's love, and knew her cousins were taking strength from their own Beasts.

"It'll be weird," Charlie said as they broke the hug. "Going back to our normal lives after all this." He stared wide-eyed at them. "We only got the Arcane Bands a couple of months ago, and since then, we've battled wizards and power-hungry scientists and all kinds of monsters."

"Not to mention saving Beast eggs," added Sam. "And travelling to entirely

different dimensions using magic portals, and inheriting a castle." He grinned. "I can't wait to tell the guys at school!"

"We can't *tell* people," said Amy. "And we have to keep our Beasts secret – at least for the time being."

"I know," laughed Sam. "I was kidding."

"Do you think the Earth is totally safe now?" wondered Charlie. "Karita did say if we were in trouble, we should contact her. Do you think she expects more bad stuff to happen?"

"I have no idea," said Amy, combing her fingers through Wuko's warm fur. "But we have Wuko and Sali and Spark, and we have our Arcane Bands." She gazed proudly into the faces of her two cousins. "And I know one other thing," she added. "We're Guardians, and we have the responsibility to protect Earth, and there isn't anything in the world we can't face, so long as we're together!"

THE END

Read all the fantastic
NEW BLOOD books!

Discover how Amy, Charlie and Sam's adventures began in BEAST QUEST: NEW BLOOD

PROLOGUE

Karita of Banquise gazed in awe at Tom, Avantia's mighty, bearded Master of the Beasts. Legendary hero and defender of the kingdom, for twenty years Tom had victoriously faced down foul creatures, powerful magical terrors and grotesque invasions from enemy realms. Among Avantia's protectors he had no equal. He was also Karita and her companions' mentor, advisor and friend.

Under his leadership, she and the others would today face their greatest challenge.

Tom pointed towards the brooding Gorgonian castle.

"We must recover the chest of Beast eggs Malvel stole," he reminded them. His fierce blue eyes moved from Karita to the others: Dell of Stonewin, whose bloodline connected him to Beasts of Fire; Fern of Errinel, linked to Storm Beasts; Gustus of Colton, bonded with Water Beasts.

"Malvel will be expecting an attack," Tom said. "His power is diminished, but he is still formidable." His eyes locked on Karita. "Stealth will be our greatest ally."

Karita felt as though her whole life

had been a preparation for this moment. Countless hours spent studying the ancient tomes, day after day of gruelling combat training, months learning how to influence the will of Stealth Beasts and control the powers that filled the Arcane Band at her wrist.

But was she ready?

She gazed into Tom's face, and her doubts faded.

Yes!

A low rumble came from the castle. Flashes of green lightning spat into the clouds as a swarm of screeching creatures erupted from the battlements.

Karita shuddered as Malvel's hideous

minions streaked through the sky toward them. They were man-sized, with dark hides, limbs tipped with hooked claws, and gaping jaws lined with sharp teeth. Their leathery wings cracked like whips.

"Karrakhs!" muttered Tom. "Karita – go!"

She nodded and slipped away behind jagged-edged rocks. She turned to see the swarm of foul creatures engulf her companions. Tom's sword flashed. Howls rang out from the Karrakhs. The Guardians were using their Arcane Bands to form weapons that spun and crushed!

Karita raced for the castle, keeping low behind the ridge of rocks. Reaching the walls, she climbed up a gnarled vine and crawled through a narrow window. She looked back again to see that Tom and the Guardians had battled their way through the castle gates.

Well fought!

She dropped into a wide room filled with bookcases and crept to the door. Torches burned in the corridor, sending shadows leaping. The castle was silent, but Karita felt a growing dread as she slipped along the walls.

She knew where the chest of Beast eggs was hidden.

But how fiercely would it be guarded?

She came to a circular room, and saw the chest standing against the wall. She was surprised not to see any of Malvel's forces in sight. *Strange* ... As she approached the chest, she checked the walls and floor for traps and other hidden dangers. Her heart hammering, Karita opened the lid and gazed down at the eggs. They were different sizes, shapes and colours. One slipped from the pile and she caught it in her gloved hand. It was pale blue, about the size of a goose egg. Acting on instinct, she slipped it inside her breastplate.

CRASH!

She spun around. Malvel stood against the room's closed door, his eyes burning.

"Did you really think you could enter my domain unseen?" he snarled, a green glow igniting in his palm. His voice was weaker than she'd imagined. "I *wanted* you to come here. After all, only a Guardian can hatch a Beast egg."

Karita swallowed hard, seeking a way to escape.

"You and your friends will hatch these Beasts and I will drink in their power," growled the wizard. "I will become mighty again and Avantia will bow before me!"

"I'm not afraid of you!" Karita shouted.

A ball of green fire exploded from Malvel's hand. Karita dived aside, seared by the heat.

She leaped up, thrusting her right arm towards the wizard. Her Arcane Band began to form a weapon, but another blast of fire sent her sliding across the floor.

Malvel loomed over her, both hands burning green. Before he could strike, the door burst open and Tom and the other Guardians rushed into the room.

"No!" roared Malvel. "Where are my Karrakhs?"

"Defeated!" shouted Tom, whirling his sword to deflect Malvel's green flames. "Guardians! Take the eggs!"

Fern dived for the chest, but a blast from the wizard knocked her off her feet.

"The eggs are mine!" howled Malvel. He traced a large circle of fire in the air. There was a blast of hot wind as the flaming hoop crackled and spat.

Malvel snatched up the chest and turned to the black heart of the fiery circle.

"He's opened a portal!" shouted Tom. "Stop him!"

Gustus ran at the wizard and seized the chest from his grip. Roaring in anger, Malvel launched a fireball, but Fern managed to shove Gustus out of its path. But the force of her push knocked Gustus into the portal. With a stifled cry, he and the chest of eggs were gone.

"No!" Fern shouted, diving in after him. With a shout, Dell ran after her.

"Wait!" shouted Tom.

"It's our duty to protect the eggs!" Dell

called back as he disappeared into the swirling portal after his two friends.

Malvel sprang forwards, but Tom bounded in front of him, holding him back with his spinning blade as the wizard hurled magical fireballs at him.

Karita noticed the walls of the portal writhing and distorting. Malvel's magical fireballs were making it unstable. At any moment it might vanish!

Tom was knocked back by a torrent of green fire as the wizard turned and leaped into the shuddering portal. Karita flung herself after him.

"No! Karita!" The last thing she heard was Tom's voice. "The portal is in flux! You could be sent anywhere!"

And then there was nothing but a rushing wind and howling darkness, as she plunged into the unknown.

*Read NEW BLOOD, Book 1
to find out what happens ...*

If you enjoyed this book, you'll love BEAST QUEST: PETORIX THE WINGED SLICER.
Read on for a sneak peek...

THE SHADOW BEAST

"Here he comes!" cried Elenna, clutching Tom's arm. "The mightiest warrior in Avantia!"

Tom frowned. "I hope I never have to face him in battle!"

They looked at each other, and both burst out laughing.

Tom and Elenna were sitting on a pair of hay bales in the courtyard of King Hugo's palace. It was a sunny afternoon, and Captain Harkman was playing with Prince

Thomas. The one-year-old baby gurgled happily as the captain hoisted him up into the saddle of an old donkey.

"Easy does it, Your Highness," grunted Harkman. He held the squirming infant firmly.

"Tommy may not be ready to guard the palace *quite* yet," said Elenna.

"Laugh while you can," said Daltec, sternly. The young magician was holding on to the donkey's reins. "Young Thomas may be Master of the Beasts one day."

"I certainly hope so," chuckled Tom. "I could do with a rest!" He darted over to take the reins from Daltec.

"All Tommy needs is a Beast to fight," said Elenna.

Daltec nodded. "Allow me..." He stepped back, lifting his hands. His fingers twitched, and a ball of green light took shape between them. Then with a sudden flash, it transformed into a tiny green dragon, no bigger than a cat. The dragon flew up above the donkey, and Prince Thomas flapped at it with his pudgy hands.

Elenna stood and bowed low. "Hail, Master of the Beasts!" she said, and everyone chuckled.

Just then, a shout came from the battlements above. "Captain Harkman, sir!" A guard was pointing his spear at something beyond the walls.

Read PETORIX, THE WINGED SLICER,
to find out what happens ...